HONK!

Pamela Duncan Edwards

Illustrated by Henry Cole

Hyperion Books for Children

New York

"Oh, no! She's at it again!" honked the goose.

"Clear a landing space!" quacked the duck.

"Guard your lily pads!" croaked the frogs.

"Watch out! Here she comes."

Mimi flew down in a perfect ballet pose.

SPLASH!

"Mimi!" cried her friends. "Stop doing that! You're driving us crazy!"

But Mimi wasn't listening. She was whirling around the pond *en pointe*.

One night many months before, Mimi had flown to a ledge at the top of the Paris Opera House and had looked down through a window. Figures twirled and leaped gracefully across a stage. Mimi had never seen anything so beautiful.

After that, she practiced every day, because Mimi
Swan had fallen in love with ballet.

In winter, a new production came to the Opera House. Mimi watched with interest.

"How pretty!" she exclaimed. "How glistening! How FEATHERY! How AMAZING!"

"What's up?" asked a pigeon.

"They're all pretending to be me!" cried Mimi in delight. "They must have noticed me practicing."

"Probably," said the pigeon. "We certainly have!"

One evening, Mimi watched the audience stepping into the Opera House.

"I wish I could sit inside the Opera House," she thought longingly.

Then Mimi became excited. "Why not?" she cried. "I'll go in right now!" Mimi picked up an old ticket stub and went up the steps.

The ticket collector's feet were hurting. She gave a yawn and reached out to take Mimi's ticket.

"HONK," said Mimi politely.

"A BIRD!" screamed the ticket collector.

"What's happening?" cried the Opera House manager, rushing forward.

"HONK!" said Mimi.

"Honk! What d'you mean, Honk?" yelled the manager. "Get out of here this instant! We can't have birds messing up our foyer. NO BIRDS ALLOWED IN THE OPERA HOUSE!"

Mimi was shocked. No one had ever shouted at her before.

A haughty lady and gentleman sauntered toward the Opera House. The gentleman flipped his cloak proudly as he passed Mimi.

"Good evening, Your Grace. Good evening, M'Lady,"
said the manager, bowing low.
"HONK," said Mimi.
"What a rude noise!" exclaimed the lady.
The haughty gentleman's ears went red. "It wasn't me," he
blustered, stepping backward into Mimi's beak.
"HONK!" said Mimi.

"You again!" roared the manager. "GET OUT! NO BIRDS ALLOWED IN THE OPERA HOUSE!"

Mimi was puzzled. "There has to be a mistake," she thought.

So Mimi tried

and tried

and tried again
to get into the Opera House.
But it was no good.

"For the last time," bellowed the manager, "go away and don't come back! No birds allowed in the Opera House!" The Opera House door slammed shut behind Mimi.

Mimi was miserable. Sadly she wandered into the darkness at the side of the Opera House and sank into the snow by the stage door. She didn't feel like practicing ever again. But just then, a figure came hurrying up the pathway muttering to itself.

"Oh, dear! I'm late again! The manager will be furious. Must hurry!"

"HONK," agreed Mimi, and she padded after the ballerina.

As the ballerina and Mimi arrived in the
wings the stage manager called,
"Cygnets—enter right."

"HONK," said Mimi happily.
"HONK?" cried the manager. "Oh, no!"
But it was too late.

Mimi was onstage.
"Great costume,"
whispered one of the
dancers.
"Love the shoes, dear,"
whispered another.
And then the music
started.

Mimi *demi-pliéd*.

She danced *en pointe*.

She *chasséd*.
Her feet flew across the floor.

She remembered everything
she had ever practiced.

The audience rose to its feet. "Who is she?"
"Where did she come from?"
"She's bewitching!"
"SHE'S A BIRD!"
"Encore," came the cry. "A marvel. Who is responsible?"

Huffing and spluttering, the manager sidled onto the stage.
A man carried out a bouquet of flowers.
"Thank you," said the manager.
"They're not for you," said the man. "They're for the bird."
The audience cheered and clapped. "Bravo!" they cried.

The manager smirked and bowed, and bowed
some more.
"Hey you, Bird," he mouthed. "Can you come again
tomorrow?"

"HONK," said Mimi.

"HONK! HONK!"

For Henry William Lloyd Edwards—
your very own book for your first birthday.
11/23/98
—P. E.

To wonderful "Mimi" and "Bitsy"
my very own prima swanerinas
—H. C.

Text © 1998 by Pamela Duncan Edwards.
Illustrations © 1998 by Henry Cole.
Hyperion Books for Children, 114 Fifth Avenue, New York, New York, 10011-5690.
Printed in the United States of America.
First Edition
1 3 5 7 9 10 8 6 4 2

This book is set in 30-point Wade Sans Light.

Library of Congress Cataloging-in-Publication Data
Edwards, Pamela Duncan.
Honk! / Pamela Duncan Edwards : illustrated by Henry Cole.—1st ed.
p.   cm.
Summary: A ballet-loving swan wins acclaim when she manages to join the other dancers in a performance of Swan Lake.
ISBN: 0-7868-0435-1 (trade)—ISBN: 0-7868-2384-4 (library)
[1. Swans—Fiction. 2. Ballet dancing—Fiction.] I. Cole, Henry, ill. II. Title.
PZ7.E26365Ho 1998
[E]-dc21   97-44260